the snow ghosts

Written and illustrated by **Leo Landry**

Houghton Mifflin Company
Boston 2003

www.houghtonmifflinbooks.com

The illustrations are watercolor and pencil on paper.

Library of Congress Cataloging-in-Publication Data is available for this title.
ISBN 0-618-19655-2

Printed in Singapore
TWP 10 9 8 7 6 5 4 3 2 1

for Mary

The snow ghosts live in the far, far north,

where snow is always falling.

Every morning when they wake up,
the snow ghosts exercise.
Up, down, up, down.

Then, as the snow falls,
they try to catch snowflakes
on their little ghostly tongues.

Some days the snow ghosts have snowball fights.
When snow ghosts throw snowballs, no one gets hit.

They even try to play with the polar bears.
But the polar bears are never interested.

It's hard to remember colors in their world of white.
If they try hard enough, some snow ghosts
can turn red, or blue, or even yellow.
Though this leaves them very tired.

Every Wednesday is snowman day.
Each snow ghost makes a snowman to put on display.
Prizes are awarded.

Saturdays are the ice-floe races.
Every snow ghost breaks off a piece of ice and jumps on.
The first to the finish line wins.

In the afternoons, the snow ghosts have fun sliding down long, icy hills of snow on their smooth ghost bellies.

On sunny days, the snow ghosts wear their sunglasses. The glare is so bright to their ghostly eyes!

And on beautiful, full-moon nights,
the snow ghosts dance about
in the light of the wintry moon.
This is their favorite time.

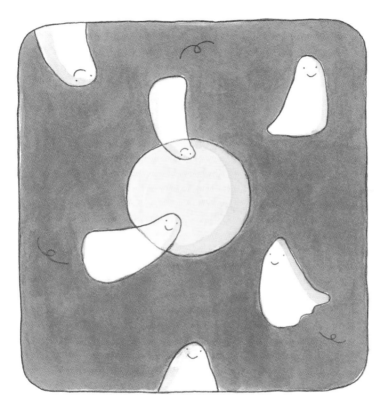

When their snowy day is over,
the snow ghosts lay their ghostly heads
on their icy beds

and dream of days to come . . .

. . . in the far, far north, where snow is always falling.